The Little Sweeties Present: A Cupcake Mystery

Written by: Arin Logan

Edited by: Laura Wenner and Arin Logan

Illustrations by: Laura Lamour

Inspired by: Bonnie

Copyright 2016 The Little Sweeties, LLC
Atlanta, GA

ISBN # 978-0-9981634-2-0 (Hardback)
ISBN # 978-0-9981634-1-3 (Paperback)
ISBN # 978-0-9981634-0-6 (Activity Book)
ISBN # 978-0-9981634-3-7 (Ebook)

For Ryan, Ruby and Mama

love, love, love

One cheery morning Ava got a mysterious itch to bake a batch of cupcakes with her sister Maisy.

The Little Sweeties have a special sense for good deeds. Their sweet atennae buzz with happy ideas.

Ava told her Mommy that something special was happening at school on Monday and cupcakes were a must.

Maisy wondered what Ava was planning. She and Rasc the sweetie dog, waited to see how they could help

Mommy went along with the plan.
She loves cupcakes too.

"Alright, my bright little bakers,
today you can be cupcake makers!"

At the store their Mommy asked,

"What flavors should we use? Chocolate or stinky shoes...."

"Ewww! Stinky shoes?"

Ava and Maisy howled with laughter.

Their Mommy is a silly lady.

Ava and Maisy looked at the colorful sprinkle options and flavor possibilities.

They grabbed the sprinkles and danced around the aisles using the shakers to make rhythmic sounds.

Chigga chigga chigga went the sprinkles and shake shake shake went the sisters! Even Mommy was dancing with delight!

Both girls wanted a different flavor, so Mommy came to the rescue and helped them compromise.

For the cake, they decided on a swirl of flavors: vanilla and chocolate. The frosting would be vanilla buttercream with orange and purple sprinkles.

Mommy helped the girls bake the cupcakes.

Swirls and sprinkles were running wild
in the happy kitchen.

Ava and Maisy ate small bites of the upcakes; a little bite here and another nibble there.

They giggled with sugary mouths and sprinkle coated hands.

Ava looked around at all of the bites missing from the cupcakes. They needed to stop nibbling and focus on packaging the cupcakes to share.

Ava told Maisy,

"We must pack up our
cupcake treats.
In class we will share
our sprinkled sweets!"

Maisy still didn't know what the surprise
was, but trusted that her sister
would tell her the mysterious plan
at pajama time.

They boxed up a bundle of cupcakes
and set a few aside
for Mommy and Daddy.

All of the sugar finally danced to a stop. It was time for bed, so the girls put on their pajamas and snuggled into cozy beds.

After Mommy and Daddy kissed them goodnight Maisy asked Ava,
"You said we are on a mission of mystery.
Can you tell me the plan of cupcake delivery?"

Ava responded,
"Maisy, I told you before.
It is something special and I cannot tell you more."

Maisy went to sleep with a "hmph", still curious
about the cupcakes. Big sisters can be so sneaky!

The next morning, Ava and Maisy dressed for school.

They ate breakfast and headed off with cupcake boxes in hand.

The girls were excited to have such a sweet gift to share.

They walked into class and placed the cupcake boxes into their cubbyholes.

The sweeties filed into the classroom as usual. Eleanor plopped down in the seat between Maisy and Ava with a sad shrug.

Ava asked why her friend Eleanor was so glum. She told them that her mom and dad were delayed getting home.

They went to visit her sick grandma, so they were not able to wish Eleanor a happy birthday.

Ava turned to Maisy and winked. Maisy then knew the reason for the cupcake mystery. Her friend Eleanor was turning 7!

Ava told Eleanor she had a wonderful surprise for her.

She said,

"Eleanor, don't be sad today. I remembered it was your birthday!"

Eleanor lit up. While hugging Ava she said,

"My parents are away and my grandma is sick.
I'm so happy to have a sweet friend,
to grant my cupcake wish."

Giddy with excitement Ava raised her hand and asked the teacher if she could share a surprise treat with the class.

The teacher agreed and let Maisy help too. They showed Eleanor the colorful cupcakes they made for her special day.

Maisy said to Eleanor,

"My sister wanted to do something nice for a friend. She kept it a mystery and now I know how the story ends."

They all enjoyed a cupcake thanks to Ava and Maisy's sweet surprise!

You can make Ava and Maisy's swirl cupcakes too! Just ask a grown-up to help you. Check out the recipe on the next page.

THE LITTLE SWEETIES' CHOCOLATE AND VANILLA MYSTERY SWIRL CUPCAKES

I cup all-purpose flour or gf flour
1 1/2 tsp baking powder
1/4 tsp salt
1/2 cup sugar
2 large eggs
1/2 cup vegetable oil
1/2 cup buttermilk
I tsp vanilla extract
1/2 cup semisweet or dark chocolate, melted

Preheat oven to 350°F. Line 10 cups in a 12-cup muffin tin with paper liners. In a medium bowl, use a fork to combine the flour, baking powder and salt. In a large mixing bowl, whisk together sugar, eggs, vegetable oil buttermilk and vanilla extract. Pour in dry ingredients and stir until combined. Be careful not to overmix.

Transfer I cup of the batter to a small bowl and stir in melted chocolate. Evenly distribute batters into prepared cupcake liners, adding a spoonful of vanilla, followed by a spoonful of chocolate, followed by a little more vanilla. Gently run a knife through the batter to give them a swirl. Bake for about 10-15 minutes, until a toothpick inserted into the center comes out clean. Cool cupcakes before frosting.

Makes 10 Cupcakes

VANILLA BUTTERCREAM FROSTING

½ cup butter (or one stick), room temperature
3 Tbsp. milk (or milk substitute)
I tsp. vanilla extract
2 ½ cups confectioners' sugar

n a large bowl, beat together butter, milk and vanilla. Gradually blend in about cups confectioners' sugar until mooth. You may need to add dditional confectioners' sugar until rosting reaches a thick, spreadable onsistency.

pe or spread frosting onto cooled upcakes. Then top the cupcakes ith sprinkles! Share with sweeties!

The Sweeties hid cupcakes throughout this book and want you to try and find them all.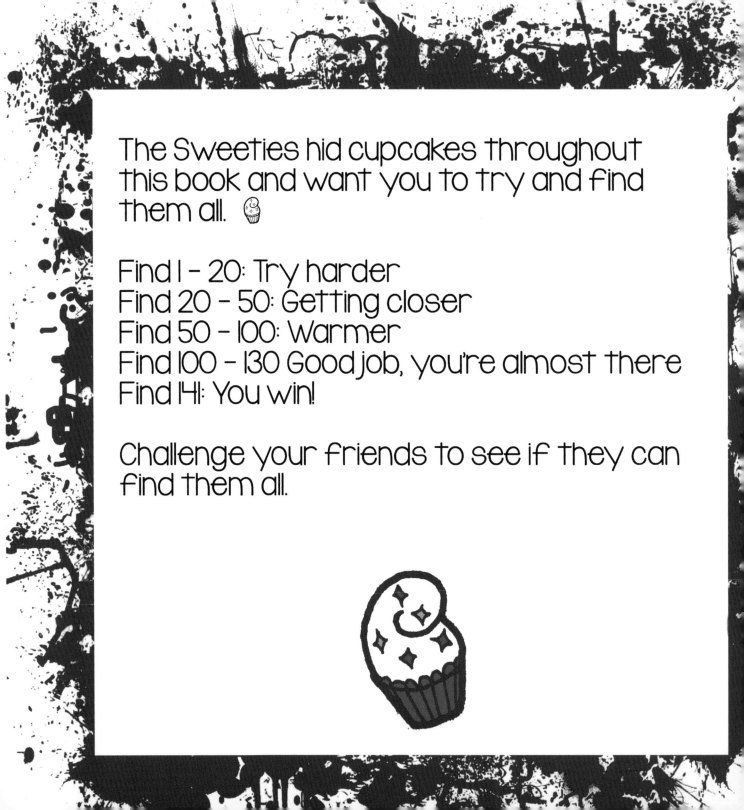

Find 1 – 20: Try harder
Find 20 – 50: Getting closer
Find 50 – 100: Warmer
Find 100 – 130 Good job, you're almost there
Find 141: You win!

Challenge your friends to see if they can find them all.

CPSIA information can be obtained at www.ICGtesting.com
Printed in the USA
LVIW01n0325211116
513661LV00002B/2